TALES FROM THE
ODYSSEY
PART ONE

This volume includes:

BOOK ONE
THE ONE-EYED GIANT

BOOK TWO
THE LAND OF THE DEAD

BOOK THREE
SIRENS AND SEA MONSTERS

The Sirens

Circe's
Island

Island of
Aeolus

Scylla

Cyclops'
Cave

Island of
the Sun God

Charybdis

Land of the Dead

Calypso's
Island

Land of the
Lotus Eaters

Oceanus

MAP OF ODYSSEUS' JOURNEY

GREECE

Ithaca

Troy

CRETE

TALES FROM THE
ODYSSEY
PART ONE

by MARY POPE OSBORNE

Disney · HYPERION
LOS ANGELES   NEW YORK

Special thanks to Frederick J. Booth, Ph.D.,
Professor of Classical Studies, Seton Hall University,
for his expert advice

The One-eyed Giant text copyright © 2002 by Mary Pope Osborne
The One-eyed Giant artwork copyright © 2002 by Troy Howell
The Land of the Dead text copyright © 2002 by Mary Pope Osborne
The Land of the Dead artwork copyright © 2002 by Troy Howell
Sirens and Sea Monsters text copyright © 2003 by Mary Pope Osborne
Sirens and Sea Monsters artwork copyright © 2003 by Troy Howell

This edition cover art copyright © 2010 by James Bernardin

First edition, May 2010
20 19 18 17 16 15 14 13 12 11
FAC-026988-16220
Printed in the United States of America
ISBN 978-1-4231-2864-9
Visit www.disneybooks.com

SUSTAINABLE FORESTRY INITIATIVE
Certified Sourcing
www.sfiprogram.org
SFI-00993

THIS LABEL APPLIES TO TEXT STOCK

For Wilborn Hampton and LuAnn Walther

CONTENTS

BOOK ONE

BOOK TWO

BOOK THREE

Book One

THE ONE-EYED GIANT

PROLOGUE

$\mathcal{I}$n the early morning of time, there existed a mysterious world called Mount Olympus. Hidden behind a veil of clouds, this world was never swept by winds, nor washed by rains. Those who lived on Mount Olympus never grew old; they never died. They were not humans. They were the mighty gods and goddesses of ancient Greece.

The Olympian gods and goddesses had great power over the lives of the humans who lived on earth below. Their anger once caused a man named Odysseus to wander the seas for many long years, trying to find his way home.

Almost three thousand years ago, a Greek poet named Homer first told the story of Odysseus' journey. Since that time, storytellers have told the strange and wondrous tale again and again. We call that story the Odyssey.

THE CALL TO WAR

ong ago on the island of Ithaca in ancient Greece, there lived a man named Odysseus. Though he was king of the island, Odysseus lived a simple life. He enjoyed tending his fields and orchards and working with his hands as a crafts-man and carpenter. More than anything, he enjoyed the company of his family— his aged mother and father; his loving wife, Penelope; and their small son, Telemachus.

One day as Odysseus was plowing his fields, he gazed for a long time at Penelope and Telemachus. The baby was sleeping in his mother's arms under a nearby tree. Odysseus imagined that someday he would teach his son to farm the land and care for the orchards. He would teach him to sail a ship around the Greek islands.

As Odysseus dreamed of his son's future, a servant ran from the palace. "A messenger from King Agamemnon has arrived!" the servant shouted.

Dread crept over Odysseus. He knew why the messenger had come. Agamemnon, the ruler of all the Greek islands, was calling for the kings and princes of Greece to wage war against the faraway city of Troy. A Trojan prince had kidnapped a Greek queen named Helen, taking her from her husband.

"Odysseus of Ithaca!" the messenger

shouted. "I bring orders for you to join King Agamemnon in the fight against Troy!"

Odysseus glared at the man, trying desperately to think of some way to avoid leaving his family. Though he was a brave warrior and leader of men, his love for his family overshadowed all else. He loathed the thought of having to leave his home.

"Odysseus!" the messenger shouted. "Remember it was you yourself who first called for our countrymen to swear to defend the marriage of Helen!"

Odysseus remembered this well.

Helen was the most beautiful woman in all the world. When she was old enough to wed, all the princes and kings of Greece had wanted to marry her. Fearing that the men's jealousies would bring their nation to ruin, Odysseus had urged them all to swear to defend Helen's marriage always, no matter who she chose for her husband.

"In the name of Agamemnon, I command you to set sail at once!" the man shouted.

Ignoring the messenger, Odysseus began to behave in a strange way. Instead of yoking two oxen together to pull his plow, he yoked an ox to a small donkey. Instead of casting seeds into the furrows of his fields, he cast salt. He hoped the messenger would think he had gone mad.

But the messenger suspected Odysseus was only pretending. To test him, the messenger snatched Telemachus from Penelope's arms and placed the baby in front of Odysseus' plow.

Penelope screamed.

Odysseus quickly turned his plow so he would not harm the boy. And in that moment, he knew he had sealed his fate. He had proved his sanity. He would now have to leave his family and answer the call to war.

THE WOODEN HORSE

$\mathcal{F}$or the next ten years, Odysseus camped with a thousand Greek warriors outside the walls of Troy. He despaired that the war would ever end. The Greeks slew many Trojan leaders in battle, including the prince who had stolen Helen from her Greek husband. But Helen herself remained captive within the thick walls of Troy. The Greeks had not been able to find a way to enter the city and take her back.

One day, Odysseus left the Greek camp and sat alone on the Trojan shore. He mourned the separation from his wife and felt terribly sad that he had missed seeing his son grow up. He feared that his mother and father might have died while he was at war, and that he would never lay eyes on them again.

Suddenly, a tall woman appeared before Odysseus. She wore a shining helmet and carried a spear and shield. The woman was Athena, the goddess of wisdom and war and a daughter of Zeus.

Athena stared at Odysseus with flashing gray eyes. Though her gaze was fierce, it was also kind. Athena had always been fond of Odysseus. She admired his skills as a carpenter and craftsman. And she loved him for his strength and clever ways.

Odysseus was speechless as he stood before the goddess.

"I have come to help you take Helen back from the Trojans," she said. "Here is how you shall bring down the walls of Troy. Direct your carpenters to build a giant wooden horse. Hide with a few of your men inside the horse while the rest of the Greeks pretend to leave the island in defeat. Thinking the horse has been abandoned, the Trojans will bring it inside their walls. When night falls and the Greek soldiers return, open the gates of the city and let them in."

The goddess then left as quickly as she had come.

Odysseus set to work at once. He called for his best carpenter and directed him to build the giant wooden horse. When the horse was finished, Odysseus ordered his men to carve Athena's name into its side. He then chose his bravest warriors and led them up a rope ladder to a secret trapdoor in the belly of the horse. He and his men locked themselves inside and waited.

Soon Odysseus heard the Greek warriors set fire to their camp. He heard them board their ships and sail away in the night.

Odysseus dared not sleep as he waited

for morning. After many hours, he heard seagulls crying in the dawn light. Then he heard footsteps on the sand and voices.

"What is this horse?" a Trojan shouted. "Why did the Greeks build it, and then abandon it on our shore?"

"It is ours now!" said another. "Let us haul it inside our walls!"

"No, we must not!" cried another. "We must never trust gifts from the Greeks! Throw this monstrous thing into the sea!"

"Burn it!" some yelled.

"Let it stay!" others shouted.

The argument was interrupted by a

Greek soldier who had stayed behind and allowed himself to be captured by the Trojans. Now he claimed to be a traitor to the Greeks.

"This horse is a gift for Athena," he lied. "See her name carved into its side? If you destroy it, the goddess will punish you. But if you give it a place of honor in your city, she will give Troy power over all the world."

The Trojans argued bitterly about whether or not to trust the captive. Finally, the king made a decision. "We will keep the wooden horse," he said.

"Bring it inside the gates of Troy."

Odysseus felt great relief and excitement. Athena's plan was working! He and his men scarcely breathed as the Trojans heaved the giant horse onto rollers, then pushed it into the city.

Odysseus waited patiently for night to come. When all was silent, he opened the trapdoor in the horse's belly.

It was pitch-black outside. The city was eerily calm. All the Trojans had returned to their homes and gone to bed.

Under the cover of darkness, Odysseus led the way down the rope ladder. He and his men crept to the city gates, unbolted them, and threw them open.

Hordes of Greek warriors were waiting on the other side! In the darkness, they had sailed back to Troy and silently gathered outside the gates.

With a horrifying battle cry, the Greek army rushed into the city. They killed many men and captured women and children to keep as slaves. They found Helen and returned her to her Greek husband.

By dawn, the entire city of Troy was in flames. The triumphant Greek warriors loaded their ships with treasure. Then finally, after ten long years, they set sail for home.

As a strong wind carried Odysseus and his twelve sleek ships away from the shores of Troy, he was jubilant. He imagined all of Ithaca rejoicing over his victorious return. He imagined himself soon embracing his beloved wife and son, and his parents. Never had he felt so hopeful and happy.

THE ODYSSEY BEGINS

$\mathcal{S}$oon after the Greek ships left Troy, the skies began to blacken. Lightning zig-zagged above the foamy sea. Thunder shook the heavens.

Mighty winds stirred the water. The

waves grew higher and higher, until they were rolling over the bows of the ships.

"The gods are punishing us!" the Greek warriors shouted. "We shall all drown!"

As his men frantically fought the storm, Odysseus felt bewildered. Why was Zeus, god of the skies, hurling his thunderbolts at them? Why was Poseidon, lord of the seas, sending great waves over the waters?

Odysseus turned to his men. "What has happened to anger the gods?" he shouted. "Tell me!"

"Before we left Troy, Greek warriors invaded Athena's temple!" said one of his men. "They were violent and disrespectful."

Odysseus was stunned. The Greeks had offended the goddess who had helped them to victory! And now her anger might drown them all.

The wind grew stronger. It whipped the sails of the Greek ships and slashed them to rags. "Lift your oars!" Odysseus shouted to his men. "Row! Row to shore!"

The Greeks struggled valiantly against the mighty wind and waves. Fighting for their lives, they finally rowed their battered ships to a strange shore. There they found shelter in a rocky cave.

The storm raged for two more days and nights. Then, on the third day, a fair wind blew, the sun came out, and the wine-dark sea was calm at last.

"Now we can continue on our way," Odysseus said to his men. "Athena is no longer angry." In the rosy dawn, he ordered them to raise their tattered sails and set off again for Ithaca.

But, alas, the wrath of Athena had not been fully spent. Hardly had Odysseus reached the open sea than another gale began to blow.

For many days, Odysseus and his men fought the wind and the waves, refusing to surrender to the storm. Finally, on the tenth day, there was sudden calm.

Odysseus ordered his fleet to sail into the cove of a leafy green island. There he hoped to find food and drink for his hungry, weary men.

The Greeks dropped anchor. Then they dragged themselves ashore. They drank cool, fresh water from a spring and collapsed onto the sand.

As Odysseus rested, he ordered three of his men to explore the island and look for provisions.

When the three had not returned by late afternoon, Odysseus grew angry. Why did they tarry? he wondered.

Odysseus set out in search of the men. He moved through the brush and brambles, calling their names.

He had not gone far when he came upon a group of peaceful islanders. They greeted him with warm, friendly smiles. And they offered him their food—lovely bright flowers.

Odysseus was famished. But just as he was about to eat the flowers, he caught sight of his missing men. The three were lying on the ground with dreamy smiles on their faces.

Odysseus called each man by name, but none of them answered. They did not even look at him.

"What have you done to them?" he asked the islanders.

"We have given them our flowers to eat," an islander answered. "This is our greatest gift. The gods would be angry if we did not offer to feed our guests."

"What sort of flowers are these?" Odysseus asked.

"They come from the lotus tree," the islander said. "They have the magical power of forgetfulness. They make a man forget the past."

"Forget his memories of home?" asked Odysseus. "And his memories of his family and friends?"

The lotus-eaters only smiled. They again offered Odysseus their sweet, lovely flowers. But he roughly brushed them away. He pulled his three men to their feet and commanded them all to return to their ships at once.

The men began to weep. They begged to be left behind so they could stay on the island and eat lotus flowers forever.

Odysseus angrily herded the men back to the ships. As they drew near the shore, the three tried to escape. Odysseus called for help.

"Tie their hands and feet!" he shouted to his crew. "Make haste! Before others eat the magic flowers and forget their homes, too!"

The three flailing men were hauled aboard and tied to rowing benches. Then

Odysseus ordered the twelve ships to push off from shore.

Once more, the Greeks set sail for Ithaca, sweeping the gray sea with their long oars. As they rowed past dark islands with jagged rocks and shadowy coves, Odysseus felt troubled and anxious. What other strange wonders lurked on these dark, unknown shores?

THE MYSTERIOUS SHORE

$\mathcal{S}$oon the Greek ships came upon a hilly island, thick with trees. No humans seemed to live there. Hundreds of wild goats could be heard bleating from the island's gloomy thickets.

Odysseus ordered his men to drop anchor in the shelter of a mist-covered bay. By the time the Greeks had lowered their sails, night had fallen. The moon was hidden by clouds. In the pitch dark, the men lay down on the sandy shore and slept.

When daylight came, the men woke to see woodland nymphs, the daughters of Zeus, driving wild goats down from the hills. The hungry Greeks eagerly grabbed their bows and spears and slew more than a hundred goats.

All day, the Greeks lingered on the island, feasting on roasted meat and drinking sweet wine. As the sun went down, they stared at a mysterious shore across the water. Smoke rose from fires on the side of a mountain. The murmur of deep voices and the bleating of sheep wafted through the twilight.

Who lives there? Who stokes those fires? Odysseus wondered silently. *Are they friendly or lawless men?*

Darkness fell, and the Greeks slept once more on the sand. When he was wakened by the rosy dawn, Odysseus stared again at the mysterious shore in the distance. Though he was yearning to set sail for

Ithaca, a strange curiosity had taken hold of him.

Odysseus woke his men. "I must know who lives on that far shore," he said. "With a single ship, I will lead an expedition to find out whether they are savages or civilized humans. Then we will continue our journey home."

Odysseus chose his bravest men to go with him. They untied a ship from their fleet and pushed off from the island.

Soon the Greeks were swinging their long oars into the calm face of the sea, rowing toward the mysterious shore.

When they drew close, they dropped anchor beneath a tall, rocky cliff.

Odysseus filled a goatskin with the best wine he had on board, made from the sweetest grapes. "This will be our gift to repay the hospitality of anyone who welcomes us into his home," he said.

He ordered some of his men to remain with the ship, then led the rest up the side of the cliff. On a ledge high above the water, they discovered a large, shady clearing. On the other side of the clearing, creeping vines hung over the mouth of a cave. The Greeks pushed past the vines and stepped inside.

The cave was filled with young goats and lambs. Pots of cheese and pails of goat's milk were everywhere. But there was no sign of a shepherd.

"Hurry!" said one of Odysseus' men. "Let us grab provisions and leave!"

"Yes! We should drive the lambs down to our ship before their master returns!" said another.

"No," said Odysseus. "We will wait awhile. . . . I am curious to see who lives here."

The Greeks made a fire and gave an

offering to the gods. Then they greedily took their fill of milk and cheese. Finally, in the late afternoon, they heard whistling and bleating.

"Ah, the shepherd returns," Odysseus said. "Let us step forward and meet this man."

But when they peered out of the cave, the Greeks gasped with horror—for the shepherd was not a man at all. He was a monster.

THE ONE-EYED GIANT

A hideous giant lumbered into the clearing. He carried nearly half a forest's worth of wood on his back. His monstrous head jutted from his body like a shaggy mountain peak. A single eye bulged in the center of his forehead.

The monster was Polyphemus. He was the most savage of all the Cyclopes, a race of fierce one-eyed giants who lived without laws or leaders. The Cyclopes were ruthless creatures who were known to capture and devour any sailors who happened near their shores.

Polyphemus threw down his pile of wood. As it crashed to the ground, Odysseus and his men fled to the darkest corners of the cave.

Unaware that the Greeks were hiding inside, Polyphemus drove his animals into the cave. Then he rolled a huge boulder over its mouth to block out the light of day and imprison his flock inside.

Twenty-four wagons could not haul that rock away, Odysseus thought desperately. *How will we escape this monster?*

Odysseus' men trembled with terror as the giant made a small fire and milked his goats in the shadowy light. His milking done, he threw more wood on his fire. The flame blazed brightly, lighting up the corners of the cave where Odysseus and his men were hiding.

"What's this? Who are you? From

where do you come?" the giant boomed. He glared at the Greeks with his single eye. "Are you pirates who steal the treasure of others?"

Odysseus' men were frozen with terror. But Odysseus hid his own fear and stepped toward the monster.

"We are not pirates," he said. "We are Greeks blown off course by storm winds. Will you offer us the gift of hospitality like a good host? If you do, mighty Zeus, king of the gods, will be pleased. Zeus is the guardian of all strangers."

"Fool!" the giant growled. "Who are

you to tell me to please Zeus? I am a son of Poseidon, god of the seas! I am not afraid of Zeus!"

Odysseus' men cowered in fear.

Polyphemus moved closer to Odysseus. He spoke in a soft, terrible voice. "But tell me, stranger, where is your ship? Near or far from shore?"

Odysseus knew Polyphemus was trying to trap him. "Our ship was destroyed in the storm," he lied. "It was dashed against the rocks. With these good men, I escaped. I ask you again, will you welcome us?"

The Cyclops stared for a moment at Odysseus. Then, without warning, he grabbed two Greeks. He smashed them against the stone floor, killing them at once. The giant tore the men limb from limb and devoured them—flesh, bones, and all.

The rest of Odysseus' men cried aloud with horror. They raised their arms to Mount Olympus, begging Zeus for help. Odysseus gathered his strength and commanded his men to be silent.

The giant washed down his gruesome

meal with a bucket of goat's milk. "There!" he said, smacking his lips. "Let that be my welcome to you."

The monster belched. Then he lay down on the floor among his fat sheep and tiny lambs. Soon he was fast asleep and snoring.

Trembling with rage, Odysseus drew his sword, ready to slay the bloodthirsty beast. But wisdom stopped him.

He took a deep breath. "We can never roll that rock away from the entrance," he said to his horror-stricken men. "If I slay the brute, we will die, too, trapped forever in his wretched lair."

Odysseus put away his weapon. He had no choice but to wait for morning— and for the giant to wake.

ODYSSEUS' PLAN

After many terrible hours, the light of dawn crept through the cracks at the mouth of the cave.

Odysseus watched the Cyclops open his eye, then heave himself up from the ground. The giant lit a fire and milked his goats. When he was done with his chores, he snatched up two more Greeks.

The terrified warriors again begged for Zeus to help them. But as before, the mighty god did not heed their cries.

Odysseus and his men watched the monster smash their two comrades against a stone wall, then devour them for breakfast.

The Greeks reeled at the horror of the sight. Again, Odysseus felt a murderous rage toward the monster, but again he fought to conceal it.

After his gory meal, Polyphemus rolled away the boulder from the mouth of the cave. He called for his flock and led them out into the sunlight. Then he rolled the mighty rock back against the entrance, trapping the Greeks inside. They could hear the monster whistling as he drove his goats and sheep down the mountain slope.

Odysseus and his men were sickened by the gruesome murder of their friends. The men moaned and wept, but Odysseus ordered them to be silent.

"Weeping will not save us," he said. "We must make a plan."

His men were too distraught to think clearly, so Odysseus paced about the cave alone, searching for a way to destroy the giant.

Peering about the shadowy cave, Odysseus caught sight of the giant's club. Made from fresh green olive wood, the club was as tall as the mast of a twenty-oared trading ship.

Odysseus seized the club and chopped off a six-foot stake. He ordered his men to carve the wood into a spike. When they were done, he honed one end until it was razor sharp.

"Now, let us draw lots to see who will help me," he said.

The men drew lots, and four were chosen to help. Odysseus told them his plan. Then he hid the stake in the shadows of the cave.

"All we can do now is wait," he said.

His men huddled together like frightened children. But as Odysseus sat and stared at the entrance of the cave, his heart grew cold and hard.

Finally, he heard the awful whistling of the monster, then the bleating of sheep.

The huge rock was rolled away. Sunlight streamed into the cave. Flocks of sheep and goats bounded in. The one-eyed giant lumbered behind them.

Once all were inside, Polyphemus again rolled the boulder against the mouth of the cave. Without even a glance at the Greeks, he stoked his fires and set about milking his goats.

The Cyclops finished his chores. Then just as suddenly as before, he grabbed two more men. He bashed them against the stone floor and ate them for supper. When he had finished his meal of flesh and bone, the one-eyed giant grinned horribly at the remaining Greeks.

Odysseus' men cried out in terror before the bloody monster.

Odysseus himself trembled with fury. But he forced himself to smile. He rose calmly and picked up his wineskin. With a steady hand, he poured sweet red wine into a wooden bowl.

"Here, sir," he said, offering the bowl to the Cyclops. "Please drink our good wine. I give it to you as a gift with the hope that you will take pity on us and help us find our way home."

The giant snatched the bowl from Odysseus and gulped down the wine.

When he was done, he held out the bowl and thundered, "MORE! MORE! Give me MORE!"

Odysseus poured more wine into the bowl, and Polyphemus gulped it all down.

"MORE!" the monster bellowed. "MORE! And tell me your name!"

Odysseus filled the bowl a third time. The giant poured it down his throat. Then he put down the bowl and began to stagger about the cave. Odysseus saw that the wine had gone to the giant's head. He knew it would soon be time to act.

"Sir, you have asked me for my name,"

said Odysseus. "I will give it to you as a gift. But you must give me a gift in return. My name is No One. That is what everyone calls me. No One."

The giant laughed cruelly.

"Ha! No One!" he said. "Thank you for your gift. Now I give you a gift in return. It is this: I will eat you and all of your men. But I will eat you last! That is my gift to you, No One. Ha-ha-ha!"

As he laughed, the giant lost his balance. He staggered back a few steps. Then he slid down the stone wall and crashed to the ground. His huge head drooped to one side. His eye closed and he began to snore. The giant's snores were so thunderous that all the milk pails rattled throughout the cave.

Odysseus moved quickly. He jammed the sharpened end of the stake into the burning embers. He beckoned to his men to stand near him. Then he pulled the stake from the fire.

"Help us, O Zeus!" Odysseus prayed.

The mighty god finally seemed to hear his prayer. As Odysseus took a deep breath, he felt a surge of strength and power.

Odysseus gave a sign. Then all together,

the men raised the stake and rammed its burning point into the giant's huge, bulging eye.

The Cyclops let out a piercing howl.

The eye hissed and sizzled.

The Greeks let go of the stake and fled to the corners of the cave.

Polyphemus pulled the spike from his eye and hurled it away from him. Blinded and groaning with pain, he fell to the floor of his cave. He bellowed for help.

All the other Cyclopes who lived on the island hurried over the dark rocks and gathered outside the cave.

"What ails you, Polyphemus?" one shouted. "Why do you break the stillness of the night with your cries? Who harms you?"

"NO ONE!" Polyphemus shouted, writhing on the floor of his cave. "No One tried to kill me! No One blinded me!"

"Well, if no one has harmed you, you must be ill," said the other Cyclopes. "And when Zeus makes one of us ill, the others can offer no help."

With no further talk, all the Cyclopes turned away and lumbered back to their own caves.

Odysseus felt laughter rise in his throat. His bold trick had worked!

Growling with rage, the giant felt along the walls with his huge hands, searching for the rock that sealed up the cave. When he found it, he pushed it away.

Odysseus was overjoyed—he and his men would soon be free! But before they could flee, the blinded Cyclops sat down in the open mouth of the cave and stretched out his huge arms. The monster grew very still. He was waiting to capture the first Greek who tried to escape.

THE CURSE OF THE CYCLOPS

*H*our after hour, Polyphemus waited at the mouth of the cave. Hour after hour, Odysseus wondered how he might save himself and his men. Near dawn, his gaze rested on the fat, fleecy sheep. *There* *must be a way to use them*, he thought.

Odysseus stood up silently. He quickly chose eighteen of the largest sheep. Then, using long, young willow branches, he silently bound the sheep together in groups of three. When this was done, he lashed each of his men to the belly of a middle sheep.

When all his men were concealed by the curly, white wool of the sheep, Odysseus chose the mightiest ram for himself and hid beneath it.

Dawn crept into the cave. Just as they did every morning, the sheep began to bleat and move out of the cave, heading for the mountain meadows.

As the sheep moved past the Cyclops, he ran his hands through their wool, searching for Odysseus' men. But the blind giant touched only the two outside sheep in the groups of three. Little did he imagine that the Greek warriors were hiding in the wool of the center sheep.

One by one, Odysseus' men passed smoothly and secretly past the Cyclops and out of his reach. But when the mighty ram began to move out of the cave, the giant stopped him and stroked his wool.

Odysseus held his breath as he hid beneath the ram's belly.

"Ah, my old friend," Polyphemus said to the ram, "why do you move so slowly this morning? You are always the first to run into the flowery meadow or the bubbling spring. You are always the first to come home at night. Do you move slowly now because you know your master has lost his sight? Do you grieve for me? If only you could speak and tell me where No One hides, I would catch him and bash out his brains."

The ram bleated impatiently, and the

giant let him go. The ram—and Odysseus—moved out of the giant's reach and beyond the cave.

As soon as they were a safe distance away, Odysseus slipped out from beneath the ram's belly. He quickly untied his men. He silently urged them to hurry. Then the men drove the giant's flock down to the water.

The Greeks who had waited by the ship rejoiced to see their friends alive. But they fell to weeping when they learned of the six who had been brutally slain.

"End your grieving now!" Odysseus

ordered. "We must put out to sea at once, before the Cyclops discovers we are gone and comes after us!"

Odysseus and his men drove the Cyclops' sheep onto their ship. Then they pushed off and rowed quickly through the calm, gray sea.

Once they were far away from shore, Odysseus stood up in the boat. "Polyphemus!" he shouted. "Polyphemus!"

In a moment, the monster appeared at the edge of the cliff. He bellowed with rage when he realized Odysseus and his men had escaped.

"You should have thought twice before making a meal of my men!" shouted Odysseus. "See how Zeus has punished you!"

The blind giant answered with a shriek of fury. He tore a slab of rock from the high cliff, and with all his might he hurled it at the Greeks.

The rock crashed into the water in front of the ship. A wave rose like a huge mountain. It scooped up the Greek ship and washed it all the way back to the Cyclopes' island and hurled it onto the beach!

Odysseus grabbed a long oar and

pushed the ship back into the water.

"Row! Row!" he shouted to his crew. "Row for your lives!"

The Greeks madly rowed their ship out to sea. As they moved far beyond the shore of the blind giant, Odysseus could not help jeering at the beast again.

"Polyphemus!" he bellowed.

His men begged Odysseus to hold his tongue. "Do not taunt the monster! He will sink our ship for certain!"

But Odysseus paid no attention to their pleas. His anger and pride were so great, he could not stop himself from making a terrible mistake: he told his true name to the giant.

"Polyphemus!" he shouted. "If anyone asks you who put out your eye, do not tell them it was No One. Tell them it was Odysseus, king of Ithaca! Odysseus, the great warrior and raider of cities! He was the one who blinded you!"

"Alas! The prophecy has come true!" boomed the giant. "Long ago, a soothsayer said a man named Odysseus would blind me. I had been waiting for someone of god-like strength. But you—you are a weakling! Come back, so I can give you a gift to prove my hospitality! To please your Zeus! So he will heal my eye!"

"Heal you?" Odysseus shouted mockingly. "Neither Zeus nor I wish to heal you, monster! I only wish to send you to the Land of the Dead!"

The giant lifted his hands and prayed to his father Poseidon, god of the seas. "Hear me, father!" he thundered. "Put a curse on Odysseus, king of Ithaca! May he never reach his home alive! If he must, may he lose his way, his ships, and all his men! May he find only sorrow and trouble on his journey!"

The Cyclops then picked up a rock even bigger than the first and hurled it at Odysseus. But this time the rock landed behind the ship, and a mountainous wave bore the Greek ship toward the goat island where the rest of the fleet waited.

Odysseus and his men were welcomed with great cries of relief. But once again joy turned to sorrow when the Greeks learned how the giant had brutally slain their friends.

As the sun went down, the Greeks feasted on mutton and wine. When night came, they lay down and slept soundly on the sand near the shore.

At dawn, Odysseus ordered his men aboard the ships. They all took their places. Then, with swift strokes, the Greeks left the goat island and headed across the rolling gray waves.

As the fleet of ships glided into the unknown, Odysseus looked about worriedly. Would the sea god Poseidon do as his monstrous son had asked? Would he punish Odysseus for blinding Polyphemus? And if so, how? And when?

THE PALACE OF THE WIND GOD

Soon Odysseus and his men came upon a great rocky island. A huge bronze fortress gleamed beyond its shore. Sounds of joyful music and laughter came from within the fortress.

"Seafarers once told me about this happy kingdom," Odysseus said to his men. "It is home to Aeolus, god of the winds. He lives with his six sons and six daughters. Night and day they feast on roasted meats and listen to the music of whistles and pipes."

"But how will they receive us?" a Greek asked fearfully. Odysseus' men were still plagued with nightmarish memories of the Cyclops.

"The wind god is a friend to Zeus," said Odysseus. "I believe he will honor the gods' command that strangers must always be greeted with kindness."

Odysseus' words proved to be true. When the Greeks climbed ashore on the rocky island, Aeolus welcomed them warmly. He even invited them to stay at his palace and visit with him and his family.

Odysseus wished to be on his way as soon as possible, but he agreed to stay on Aeolus' island for a month. His men greatly needed to rest, and Odysseus had an idea of how the wind god might later help them get home.

In the following weeks, while his men

enjoyed the luxurious palace life, Odysseus told the wind god the story of the long war between the Greeks and the Trojans. He told him about the wooden horse and the fall of Troy.

Aeolus was grateful to hear such exciting tales. When Odysseus finished his stories, the god offered to give him a gift in return.

"I ask only one thing," Odysseus said. "Will you help my fleet of ships get home safely to Ithaca? Will you spare us gales and storms and give us a gentle wind to open our sails?"

Aeolus enthusiastically agreed. He called together all the winds from the east and the west, and all the winds from the north and the south. At the god's bidding, each of the winds became perfectly still. Even fierce storm winds obeyed their master's command.

Aeolus bundled all the world's winds into a sack made of oxhide, so none could hinder the Greek ships from sailing home. He left out only a gentle west wind that would carry them swiftly to Ithaca.

The wind god tied the sack of winds with a silver cord and gave the bundle to

Odysseus. Odysseus hid the sack in the hollow of his ship. He did not tell his men what was inside, for he did not want them to become lazy in their efforts to return home.

Odysseus bade farewell to the family of the wind god. Then with the help of the gentle west wind, he and his men pushed off from the rocky island.

In the days that followed, the Greek fleet kept a safe, steady course. Odysseus was so excited to be returning to his family that he could not sleep. For nine days and nights, he kept watch as the salty breeze swelled the sails of his ships.

On the tenth day, in the distance, he finally saw the wooded hills that rose from the rocky shores of Ithaca. Odysseus rejoiced. He was home! The curse of the Cyclops had come to nothing!

As the Greek ships drew closer to the island, Odysseus could see the smoke of cooking fires. Was Penelope, his beloved wife, preparing dinner for their son? The boy would be ten now, an age when he would most need a father. And were Odysseus' aging parents still alive? He prayed that they would be waiting to greet him.

The balmy west wind, the gentle waves, weariness—all soon lulled Odysseus into a deep sleep.

While he slept, some of his men began to grumble to one another.

"What is inside the sack that the wind god gave our captain?"

"I imagine it is filled with splendid gifts—gold and silver."

"Why is it only Odysseus who receives the wind god's gifts? We do all the work and receive nothing."

"Quick! Before he wakes, let us search the ship and find what he hides from us!"

And so the faithless men searched the ship and found the wind god's gift. They untied the silver threads of the ox-hide sack.

Suddenly, the mighty winds of the world rushed out and swirled into a hurricane. The storm picked up the twelve ships and sent them flying wildly over the seas, far away from the shores of Ithaca.

Odysseus leaped up from his sleep and frantically tried to change the ship's course, but it was too late. He could not fight the wild winds that his men had set free.

In great despair, Odysseus thought of hurling himself into the sea. But he clung to the mast of his ship as the winds of the storm swept his fleet back the way they had come—all the way back to the island of the wind god.

Once ashore, Odysseus ran to the god's bronze fortress. He found Aeolus feasting at the banquet table with his twelve children.

Ashamed to present himself, Odysseus stood in the back of the hall, waiting to be noticed.

One of Aeolus' sons was the first to see

him. "What has happened, Odysseus?" he called out. "Why have you returned?"

Odysseus stepped forward. He told Aeolus what his men had done. "I beg you to help us again to sail home," he said. "Will you again bundle the storm winds and give us the gentle west wind to ease our course?"

"No, Odysseus," said the wind god in a low, angry voice. "You were cursed by the Cyclops. And now, indeed, the gods punish you. We can help you no more."

Odysseus looked to the children of Aeolus, hoping to find pity. But they only stared at him in cold silence.

"Begone now!" said the wind god, "before we are punished for helping you. Leave this island at once!"

Odysseus knew the wind god spoke the truth: the curse of the Cyclops was truly upon him. The gods were punishing the Greeks for blinding Poseidon's monstrous son.

Odysseus returned to his men and ordered them to put out to sea. Ashamed of their foolish act, the men rowed valiantly. But with no wind to help, their ships drifted on the sea day after day.

As Odysseus stared at the hazy horizon, grief threatened to break his spirit. But each time he thought of Penelope and Telemachus, the fire of his determination to return to Ithaca was rekindled.

I will find my way back to my family again, he promised himself. And he leaned toward the horizon, yearning for home.

EPILOGUE

While Odysseus longed for home, his wife, Penelope, longed for his return. Over the years, news had often come to Ithaca of the fate of warriors who had been slain by the Trojans—or who had died at sea returning from the war. No word, though, had ever come to the island about the fate of Odysseus.

Most people on the island assumed that

Odysseus had died in battle or a ship-wreck. Odysseus' mother had despaired of ever seeing him again and had taken her life. In his grief and despair, Odysseus' father had withdrawn to the country and lived in seclusion.

But to everyone's amazement, Odysseus' wife held fast to the belief that her husband was still alive. Every day, as she wove cloth at her loom, she frequently glanced up, as if to catch sight of him walking in the door.

Penelope most strongly sensed Odysseus' presence when she looked upon their son, Telemachus. As the boy grew older, he reminded her more and more of his father: tall and handsome, clever and brave. The boy often asked to hear stories about Odysseus. A thousand times, he imagined his father's ship sailing over the horizon.

Penelope and Telemachus had no idea that Odysseus had been so close to them the night of the great storm. It was just as well. Sadly, neither mother nor son would lay eyes upon Odysseus for many more days, months . . . or even years to come.

Book Two

THE LAND OF THE DEAD

ISLAND OF THE CANNIBAL GIANTS

$\mathcal{F}$or days, Odysseus, king of the Greek island of Ithaca, rowed with his warriors over the calm sea. As he rowed, Odysseus felt great pity for his men. He knew they grieved for their comrades murdered by the one-eyed monster, the Cyclops. He knew they also felt terrible guilt, for their foolish actions had made the wind god angry. And now there was no wind to fill the sails of the twelve Greek ships.

Odysseus shared the despair of his men. But he fought his grief with a single vision—the vision of home. Before they had angered the wind god, the Greeks had sailed close to Ithaca. For the first time in ten years, Odysseus had seen the rocky shores of his island—its green woods and the smoke of its hearth fires. He'd imagined his wife, Penelope, cooking dinner for his aged parents and his young son, Telemachus.

Now, with Ithaca and his beloved family ever in mind, Odysseus rowed. For six days and six nights, without the help of a single breeze, he and his men rowed without stopping.

On the seventh day, the Greeks came upon a mysterious land. They steered their ships toward a cove surrounded by a steep wall of cliffs, making it a natural harbor.

The Greeks sailed into the harbor

through a narrow passage. They tied their ships together near the shore. Though the waters were calm and peaceful, Odysseus felt a strange foreboding. He ordered the crew of his own ship not to moor their vessel with the others, but to anchor it near the mouth of the cove.

When the Greeks had gone ashore, Odysseus climbed a rock to look out over the strange land. He saw the smoke of a fire rising in the distance. *Who lives here?* he wondered.

He quickly returned to his men and

ordered three of them to climb over the cliffs and explore the land.

"Find out who lives here," he said. "Tell them we wish them no harm."

The three scouts set out at once. Odysseus and the others waited on the rocky shore for their return.

The men had not been gone long when horrible screams filled the air. Two of the scouts charged down the side of the mountain. Shrieking and waving their arms, they appeared to have gone mad.

"What has happened?" Odysseus shouted.

In trembling voices, the men told their terrible tale.

"We met a girl at a spring—she invited us to go with her," one said. "When we entered her house, her mother appeared— a hideous giantess—"

"Tall as a mountain!" cried the other. "She sent for her husband—another giant—a cannibal!"

The men broke down, sobbing. They told how the cannibal giant had snatched up their friend and eaten him before their very eyes.

A roar then shook the harbor like thunder.

Odysseus looked up and saw a legion of giants standing at the top of the cliffs.

The bloodthirsty cannibals began picking up huge rocks. They hurled them down the mountainside.

"Board the ships!" Odysseus called to his men. "Set sail at once!"

As the other Greeks scrambled onto their ships, Odysseus and his crew ran toward the mouth of the cove where Odysseus' black ship was moored.

The rest of the fleet was doomed. The giants hurled their rocks down upon the ships docked in the harbor. The rocks smashed the vessels to splinters and crushed many of the sailors to death.

As the Greeks screamed in agony, the cannibals raced down to the shore and speared men as if they were catching fish for supper.

Watching with rage and horror, Odysseus knew he could save only the men aboard his own ship. He drew his sword and slashed the anchor rope.

"Row! Row with all your might!" he shouted to his men. "Row for your lives!"

As the screams and cries of their comrades filled the air, Odysseus and his crew frantically rowed away from the cove of the cannibal giants.

A GIFT FROM THE GODS

Odysseus and his men rowed until their ship was finally safe upon the open seas.

As Odysseus stared at the wine-dark waves, the screams of the dying men still rang in his ears. He realized the curse of the Cyclops was coming true. He remembered the cruel words of the hideous monster: "May Odysseus never reach his home alive! May he lose his way, his ships, and all his men! May he find only sorrow and trouble on his journey!"

Odysseus had lost nearly all his ships now, and he had lost nearly all his men. Eleven vessels had been destroyed by the cannibal giants. All but forty-five of his warriors had been slain.

Stunned by their losses, Odysseus and his crew could not speak. They sailed on in silence, shaken by the memory of the giants spearing the helpless wounded.

Finally, the black ship came upon an island covered with thickets and dense woods. The Greeks climbed ashore and collapsed on the rocky beach.

For two days and two nights, Odysseus and his men lay on the hard ground, mourning their lost comrades.

On the third day, when rosy dawn crept over the island, Odysseus gathered his strength and stood up. He did not wake his crew, for he knew they had lost all heart.

They are too stricken with grief to hunt for

food, he thought. *Soon they will be too weak to sail, and they will die on this island.*

Desperate to save his men, Odysseus picked up his sword and spear. Then he set out in search of game.

Odysseus climbed a craggy hill and looked about for signs of life. In the distance, he saw smoke rising from the green forest. It curled above the trees and drifted into the sky. *Did more giants and monsters live on this shore?* Odysseus wondered anxiously. *Or might the inhabitants be welcoming and kind?*

Before Odysseus could answer these

questions, he knew he must find food for his men.

The gods seemed to hear Odysseus' thoughts—for just then, from out of the trees walked a giant stag with towering antlers.

Odysseus hurled his spear, killing the stag at once. He then fashioned a rope from willow twigs and tied the legs of the stag together. He hoisted the stag onto his shoulders and carried it back to the Greek camp.

Odysseus found his men huddled in a circle, their cloaks wrapped around their heads. Still deep in mourning, they wept bitter tears for their fallen shipmates. They trembled for their own fate as well.

"Listen, my friends," said Odysseus. "You and I shall not go down to the Land of the Dead this morning. It is not our day to die. Until that day comes, we must take care of ourselves. Rise. Be well. Let us feast on this gift from the gods."

The men uncovered their heads. They admired the mighty stag Odysseus had slain for them, and slowly they began preparing for their feast.

They washed their hands and faces in the sea. After many days of grief and suffering, their hearts began to mend.

THE WITCH'S SPELL

All afternoon, Odysseus and his crew feasted on deer meat and wine. When the sun set and darkness covered the island, they lay down on the shore and slept peacefully.

At dawn, Odysseus roused his men.

"Friends, I do not know where we are," he said. "I know only that we are on an island. Yesterday morning, when I went hunting, I climbed a hill and saw the sea all around us. I know that others live here, for I saw smoke rising from the heart of the forest—"

Before Odysseus could go on, his men cried out. They feared that more horrors like the Cyclops and the cannibal giants might await them on this strange shore.

"Harness your fears!" Odysseus commanded. "We have no choice but to explore this island. We know not where we are or how to find our way home. We must seek help from strangers."

Odysseus' men paid no heed to his words. They only grew more anxious. Before they surrendered completely to their terror, Odysseus came up with a plan.

"Listen to me," he said. "We will form two groups. I will be captain of one, and brave Eurylochus will be captain of the other."

Odysseus quickly divided his men. Twenty-two Greeks were placed under his own command, and twenty-two under that of his trusted warrior, Eurylochus.

"Now Eurylochus and I will cast lots to see which of us will explore the island," said Odysseus.

Odysseus and Eurylochus cast lots in a helmet. The lot fell upon Eurylochus. He had no choice but to lead his men into the heart of the green forest.

With great dismay, twenty-two Greeks lined up behind Eurylochus. Some wept as they marched away through the shadowy trees, fearing their impending death.

The Greeks who stayed behind wept as well. So many of their friends had already been slain that they readily imagined they might soon lose more.

Hour after hour, Odysseus waited for the return of Eurylochus and his band of men. He watched the shadows of the forest and listened for their voices. He feared he might have made a great mistake by forcing them to set out on their quest. But he dared not share his fears with the men who had remained behind.

As the sun was setting over the island, Odysseus finally heard the tramping of feet. Eurylochus burst from the trees. He was alone. His eyes were wide with terror.

Odysseus and the others rushed forward to hear his story. But Eurylochus collapsed on the ground, shaking and moaning, unable to speak.

Odysseus grabbed him by the shoulders and pulled him to his feet. "Where are the others?" he cried. "Why did you leave them?"

Eurylochus could not answer.

Odysseus shook him again. "Tell us!" he demanded. "Are they dead?"

"No—not dead," said Eurylochus. "Worse! Worse than dead—" He broke down, weeping.

"Tell us what happened!" Odysseus demanded again.

In a shaky voice, Eurylochus told his tale: "We traveled through the forest until we came to a valley. We saw a gleaming stone wall. We stepped through a gate into a clearing, and soon came face-to-face with huge wolves and mountain lions with long, sharp claws!"

"You were attacked by these wild creatures?" Odysseus asked.

Eurylochus shook his head. "They did not attack us," he said. "The wolves licked us and whined like pet dogs. The lions gently pawed us and mewed like house cats. It was strange and unnatural. We should have turned back—"

Eurylochus trembled and covered his face. But Odysseus shook him again. "Go on with your tale," he ordered. "Tell us what happened next."

Eurylochus continued. "We were frightened to be greeted so strangely by these creatures," he said. "We moved quickly past them to the inner courtyard of a palace. A voice rang out from a window—a woman singing. She had the most beautiful voice I have ever heard."

"Who was she?" asked Odysseus.

"I do not know," said Eurylochus. "When we peered through the window, we saw a radiant being weaving at a loom. She looked like a goddess. She had long braids that shone in the sunlight. Her gown was made of jewels that seemed to change colors as she sang. She wove a cloth made from the most delicate silken thread.

"I wanted to lead us away at once, for I thought of all the terrible dangers we had faced on our journey. But I alone seemed worried. The others called out to her, and she came to her door and invited them in. I held back, hiding, while they rushed forward to enter her home. I could not stop them—they followed her into her house, and she closed the door behind them.

"Peering secretly through a window, I saw her offer them food and wine. Then she turned her back on them, and she mixed a potion of pale honey and wine. As she poured this into their food, I called out to warn them. I feared she was trying to drug them. But the men seemed not to hear—they swallowed her potion willingly.

"In an instant, they were transformed. They knew not where they were or how they'd gotten there. They could not remember one another's names—or even their own. While they were in this state, the woman tapped each of them with a wand. And suddenly, they—"

Eurylochus trembled at the memory.

He hid his face, and a chill went through Odysseus. What horrible thing had the witch done to his men?

Eurylochus looked up at Odysseus. He caught his breath, then finished his dreadful tale.

"Bristles sprang out all over each man's body," he said. "They began to snort and grunt like pigs. Their heads turned into pigs' heads."

The Greeks cried out and drew back in horror.

"The enchantress then herded the pigmen into a pigsty," Eurylochus said. "She threw acorns and butternuts to the ground, and they greedily gobbled them up like . . . like swine in a farmyard!"

For a long moment, Odysseus stared at Eurylochus in silence. Finally, he spoke calmly and decisively. "Take me there," he said. "Show me the way."

Eurylochus cried out in anguish. He threw himself at Odysseus' feet and begged for his life.

"No, no! Never again!" he cried. "Let us escape this cursed island now—before the she-monster bewitches us all!"

Odysseus saw that he could not calm

Eurylochus' fears. But neither could he abandon his comrades trapped in the pigsty of the beautiful witch.

"Very well, stay here and rest with the others," he said. "In truth, I am the leader of all the Greeks on this island. I must save my men. I will find the way alone."

THE MESSENGER GOD

Odysseus slung his bronze sword over his shoulder. His men watched with great distress as he left their camp and headed off into the woods.

Odysseus walked through the quiet

green forest, through shadow and light, past gnarled trees and dense brush, until finally he came to the valley. In the distance rose the gleaming stone walls of the witch's palace.

Odysseus halted. For a moment, he thought of turning back. But he quickly gathered his strength and moved boldly toward the gate.

Suddenly a young man stepped into his path.

Odysseus started to reach for his sword. But in an instant, he realized this was no ordinary human. The man was radiant. He shone with a light so bright that Odysseus was forced to looked away.

"Your courage is admirable, Odysseus," said the stranger. "But do you know who your enemy is? Have you never heard of Circe the enchantress, daughter of the sun and the sea?"

Odysseus sighed with despair. He had indeed heard of Circe the enchantress. He knew that as a mortal, he had no power to escape her charms. Once he entered her palace, he would certainly be put under a spell like the rest.

"Do not despair, Odysseus," said the

stranger. "I have come to help you conquer Circe and free your men. Will you not trust Hermes?"

Odysseus looked up. Could this truly be Hermes, the messenger god of Mount Olympus, son of Zeus, and protector of heroes and travelers?

"I bring a charm to protect you from the witch's spell," said Hermes.

"What is it?" breathed Odysseus.

"A special herb, impossible for humans to unearth," said Hermes. "Only the gods can take it from the ground."

The god reached into a bag and pulled

out a black-rooted herb with a flower as white as milk.

"The gods call the flower *moly*," he said. "Eat the moly, and it will protect you from anything that Circe gives you to eat or drink. When she taps you with her wand, draw your sword and make her swear an oath not to harm you."

Hermes handed the black-rooted herb to Odysseus. Then, without a word, the shining god turned and disappeared back into the green forest.

Odysseus stared after Hermes in wonder. Until now on his journey,

Odysseus had only angered the gods—
the warrior goddess, Athena; the sea god,
Poseidon; and the wind god, Aeolus.
Were the gods looking upon him with
favor again?

Odysseus looked down at the magic
moly in his hands. He raised the flower to
his lips and ate it. Then, with new
strength and courage, he walked toward
the gleaming walls of the witch's palace.

THE WITCH'S PALACE

*O*dysseus opened the gate that led to Circe's palace. Huge wolves and lions prowled the courtyard. The animals approached him eagerly, sniffing the air and making soft, friendly sounds.

Odysseus stared at them with horror and pity. He knew that they were men trapped in the bodies of wild creatures.

Odysseus moved swiftly through the courtyard. At the door of the palace, he called out for Circe.

Soon the enchantress appeared. Her long braids gleamed like gold. Her jeweled gown shimmered and sparkled.

She spoke in a soft, warm voice. "Enter, please," she said to Odysseus, and she held open the door.

Without a word, Odysseus stepped

into the sunlit palace. Circe invited him to sit down and rest.

"Let me make a drink to refresh you after your long travels," she said.

She left the room for a moment. Then she came back with a cup, and she handed it to Odysseus.

"Here," she said. "Drink this."

Odysseus put the cup to his lips. As he sipped the brew, Circe tapped him with her wand.

"Foolish man!" she said. "Off to the pigsty with the rest of them!"

Hermes' magic herb protected Odysseus

from Circe's evil spell. He did not turn into a pig as the witch had expected. Instead, he pulled out his bronze sword and held it to her throat.

Circe shrieked in alarm. "Why does my magic have no effect on you?" she cried. "Who are you? What is your name?"

"My name is Odysseus," he told her.

"Odysseus!" she said. "Hermes once told me that a great warrior named Odysseus would someday visit my palace. If you are indeed this man, put away your sword! We must trust one another and become friends."

Odysseus glared at her. "How can you speak of trust when your evil magic has transformed my men into beasts? You must swear an oath that you will do nothing to harm me."

Circe bowed her head. In a whisper she swore not to harm Odysseus. When Odysseus put his sword away, she called for her handmaidens.

Lovely nymphs of the woods and rivers slipped out from the shadows of the palace. They made a great fire under a huge cauldron of water.

Odysseus bathed in the soft, healing

waters. Then he dressed in a flowing cloak. The nymphs led him to the great hall of the palace where a feast had been prepared for him.

Circe invited Odysseus to sit at her table. She filled their golden cups with wine.

But Odysseus would not eat or drink. He sat in silence, staring at Circe.

"Odysseus, why will you not eat my bread or drink my wine?" she asked. "You must not fear me now, for I have given my solemn oath that I will never harm you."

Odysseus fixed his eyes upon her.

"What sort of captain could enjoy meat or wine when his men are not free?" he asked. "If you want me to be happy at your table, you must undo the spell you have cast over my men."

Circe held his gaze for a long moment. Then she took a deep breath and rose from the table. With her wand in her hand, she stepped out of the palace into the courtyard.

Odysseus followed her and watched her open the gate to the pigsty. Twenty-two fat pink hogs barreled forward, snorting and grunting.

The enchantress rubbed a potion on the head of each animal, then touched them all with her wand. All at once their bristles fell off, and the pigs miraculously turned back into men. The men were younger, taller, and more handsome than ever before. They embraced Odysseus and wept with joy. They asked about their comrades.

Even Circe was moved by the tears of her captives. "Odysseus, go back to the rest of your crew. Bring them to my palace," she said. "I swear that I will treat them well, too."

Odysseus left the palace. He hurried through the green forest until he came to the men waiting for him on the shore. When they saw their leader alive, they shouted with great relief and threw their arms around him.

"With the help of Hermes, the spell of Circe, the enchantress, has been broken," said Odysseus. "Your comrades have all been turned back into men. Come with me now to the palace and you shall be united with them."

Some of the Greeks drew back in fear.

"I assure you," Odysseus told them

gently, "Circe has sworn to welcome you into her palace."

All the men finally agreed to go with Odysseus. They pulled their ship onto the shore and hid all their belongings in a cave. Then they followed Odysseus back through the shadowy green forest until they came to Circe's glimmering palace.

Circe welcomed the Greeks into her palace. She bid her handmaidens to draw baths for the men and anoint them with olive oil. The nymphs gave the tired Greeks woolen cloaks and tunics, then led them to a feast in the great hall.

At the feast, Circe urged Odysseus to remain with her in her palace. "You are not the same man you were when you left Ithaca long ago," she said. "Your battles and sorrows have left you weak and weary. Your own family will not know you."

Odysseus did indeed feel a great weariness as he thought of the war with Troy and his nightmarish voyage toward home—the monsters and giants, the cruel deaths of his men.

"Stay with me until you have forgotten all your grief and sad memories," said

Circe. "When you are strong in mind and body, I will help you find your way home."

Feeling the burden of his losses, Odysseus surrendered to the wishes of the lovely witch. He promised Circe he would stay with her until he and his men were strong again.

ANOTHER JOURNEY

$\mathcal{I}$n the days that followed, Odysseus and his men enjoyed the warmth and luxury of Circe's palace. They rested and ate good meat and drank sweet wine.

As they refreshed themselves on the

enchanted island, time passed swiftly. The days turned into weeks, and the weeks into months. After a full year, Odysseus' men came to him.

"Should we not leave this palace soon?" one asked.

"Have you forgotten Ithaca?" said another. "Shall we never see our homeland again?"

Odysseus' heart was stirred by the words of his men. He thought of home—of Penelope and Telemachus, and of his mother and father. A great yearning to see them rose up in him.

He hurried to Circe's chambers.

"My men and I are strong again thanks to your kindness," he said. "But remember the promise you made me? You said you would help us return safely to Ithaca, once we had rested and regained our strength."

"And I shall," said Circe. "But you must take another journey first. You must seek counsel from Tiresias, the blind prophet of Thebes. Tiresias sees the future. Only he can tell you how to get home."

"But Tiresias of Thebes is dead," said Odysseus, puzzled.

"Yes, Tiresias is dead," said Circe, "but he still has all the wisdom he had on earth."

"I do not understand," said Odysseus. "How can one who lives in the Land of the Dead give counsel to a living man?"

"You must travel to the Land of the Dead," said Circe. "There you will speak to the ghost of Tiresias."

Odysseus could not speak. It seemed an unbearable terror for a living man to visit the dark world ruled by the god Hades, and his queen, Persephone.

"No man has ever found the Land of the Dead," he said in a hushed voice.

"Only the spirits know how to travel there. What ship will take me? What wind will blow?"

"You cannot travel all the way there in your ship," said Circe. "The North Wind will take you to the edge of the sea, to Oceanus, the river that circles the world. Once you have sailed across Oceanus, you may enter the Land of the Dead."

"What must I do then?" Odysseus asked.

"You must disembark from your ship and travel on foot through a grove of willows and poplars," said Circe. "When you come to the place where two rivers meet—the River of Groans and the River of Flame—dig a trench. Pour honey, milk, wine, and white barley meal into it, as gifts to the spirits of the dead. Then sacrifice two sheep and pour their blood into the trench. After you have done this, stand guard until the ghost of Tiresias appears. Allow him to drink from the trench, and he will tell you how to find your way home to Ithaca."

Odysseus bowed his head. He knew he could not avoid this dreadful journey if he wanted to see his home and family again.

He tried to gather his courage, as he so often ordered his men to do. He looked up at Circe and nodded.

Then, without another word, Odysseus pulled on a fine cloak and strode through the palace, waking each of his men.

"Rise now," Odysseus said. "We must leave this place today."

The men were relieved, for they imagined they were about to set sail for home. But when the Greeks had gathered outside the palace, Odysseus revealed their true destination.

"Soon we will set sail for Ithaca," he

said. "But first we must go on another journey. We must travel to the Land of the Dead. There I will speak with the ghost of the wise prophet Tiresias."

The men cried out in protest. But Odysseus told them he had no choice.

"Only Tiresias can tell me how to find the way home," he said. "Please, come with me. Give me company on my journey to the Land of the Dead."

Their heads bowed in anguish, the men followed their leader down to their ship. They climbed aboard. They hoisted their sails and pushed out to sea.

As the black ship sailed over the waves, Odysseus felt a gust of warm gentle wind. He sensed that Circe was close by.

The enchantress sent fresh breezes all day. She filled the sails of the black ship and sent it flying over the waves.

THE LAND OF THE DEAD

*W*hen the sun had gone down and darkness had fallen, Odysseus and his men
arrived at the edge of the sea. They sailed
through a gray mist into the deep waters of
Oceanus, the river that flows around the

world. Then they sailed across Oceanus and finally came to the Land of the Dead.

The Greeks moored their vessel on a dark riverbank shrouded in fog. As they stared into the mist, the men shook with terror, afraid to venture into the haunted realm. Odysseus himself trembled at the thought of what lay ahead. But with firm resolve, he stepped ashore and ordered his men to follow him with two sheep from Circe's island.

Odysseus and his men traveled on foot through a grove of poplars and willows. They stopped when they came to the place where two rivers met, the River of Flame and the River of Groans.

There, in a place never touched by the rays of the sun, Odysseus dug a deep trench. He poured in the mixture of honey, milk, wine, and white barley meal. He offered prayers for the spirits of the dead. Then he ordered his men to slay the two sheep as a sacrifice to the gods.

As soon as Odysseus poured the blood of the sacrificed animals into the trench, ghostly beings appeared out of the mist— the spirits of old men and women, the spirits of warriors still wearing their armor, the spirits of young women who had mourned for their lost men and died of broken hearts.

Thousands of ghosts began moving slowly toward the Greeks. Drawn to the scent of the blood, they made strange wailing noises.

Odysseus' men shook and trembled. Odysseus himself turned pale with fear. But he drew his sword to keep the spirits away until the ghost of Tiresias, the blind prophet, appeared.

While Odysseus fiercely guarded the trench, his gaze came to rest on one of the spirits floating through the mist. With shock and horror, he recognized someone he loved very dearly.

Moving toward him was the ghost of his own mother.

LIKE A SHADOW OR A DREAM

Odysseus wept. He had not seen his mother for more than ten years, not since he had left Ithaca. He knew now that one of his worst fears had been realized—while he had been away, his beloved mother had died.

He called her name. But the spirit of his mother did not speak to him—she did not seem even to recognize him. She seemed only to yearn for a taste of the sheep's blood in the trench.

In spite of his great sorrow, Odysseus held up his sword and would not let his mother's ghost come closer. He kept guarding the trench, waiting for the spirit of Tiresias to appear.

At last a frail figure drifted out of the mist. Carrying a golden scepter in his hand, the ghost of an old man moved through the swirling gray air toward the animal blood. Odysseus lowered his sword and allowed the spirit of Tiresias to drink from the trench.

Once the ghost had had his fill of the sheep's blood, he rose and turned to Odysseus. In a clear, cold voice, he said:

"Odysseus, you have come to ask me about your journey home. The gods are making your voyage very difficult. They will not allow you to escape the anger of Poseidon for blinding his son, the Cyclops."

Odysseus felt a wave of despair. The

curse of the Cyclops seemed too terrible for him to endure.

"Do not lose hope," the ghost said. "You may still return to Ithaca. But you must heed my warning. On your way home, you will pass the island of the sun god. On this island there are many beautiful sheep and cattle. Do not let your men touch even one of these creatures. They are much adored by the sun. Any man who tries to slay them will meet his doom."

Odysseus nodded.

"Tell your men to leave these herds

untouched and think only of returning home," the ghost said. "If they do not obey this command, they will die, and your ship will be destroyed. You alone might escape. But if you do, you will be a broken man. And you will find great trouble in your house."

Odysseus was grateful for the wise man's warnings. He resolved to keep his men from touching the cattle and sheep of the sun god.

"Many years from now, death shall come to you from the sea," the ghost of the soothsayer said finally. "Your life shall leave you when you are old and have found peace of mind."

Odysseus nodded. "If this is the will of the gods, so be it," he said. As Tiresias started to move away, Odysseus called after him. "Wait, please, before you leave—"

The ghost turned back.

"Can you tell me why my mother's spirit does not speak to me when I call her name?" Odysseus asked.

"Your mother's ghost can speak only if you allow her to taste the blood in the trench," answered the ghost of Tiresias.

"Until then, she has not life enough to speak."

The spirit of the wise prophet turned away and Odysseus watched him fade back into the mist.

Odysseus then bid his mother's ghost to come forward and taste the blood from the trench.

Once she had tasted the sheep's blood, the spirit of Odysseus' mother seemed to gain strength. When she looked again at her son, she cried out in surprise.

"My beloved!" she said. "You are not a spirit! Why are you here?"

Odysseus gently explained to his mother the reason for his journey to the Land of the Dead. Then he asked her many questions: "How are Penelope and Telemachus? Did Penelope bury my memory and marry another? How is my father? Is he still alive?"

The ghost looked at her son sadly.

"Your family has been broken by sorrow," she said. "Your wife still waits for you. But she spends her days and nights weeping. Your son is strong and brave. Though he is young, he guards your home, your fields, and your livestock. He also mourns your absence, as does your father. Your father lives in the country and never goes near town. In winter, he wears only rags and sleeps on the floor. In summer, he sleeps in the vineyard. He weeps for you all the time."

Odysseus was grieved to hear this news of his family. "And you, Mother?" he asked. "What sad fate has befallen you?"

"Your absence weighed too greatly on my heart," she said. "As I grew more and more certain you would never return home, I became too sad to live."

Odysseus reached out to embrace his mother's ghost. Three times he tried. But each time, she slipped away from him as if she were made of air.

"Mother!" he cried. "Why are you not there when I try to embrace you?"

"My son, I am only a spirit," she said gently. "Leave the Land of the Dead, now. Find the light of day while you still live."

To Odysseus' great sadness, the spirit of his mother then faded from his sight, like a shadow or a dream.

THE WARRIOR GHOSTS

*W*hen the ghost of Odysseus' mother had gone, more spirits came forward to drink from the trench.

Odysseus drew his sword and ordered them to approach one at a time.

First came the spirits of the wives and the mothers of slain Greek heroes. Then came the ghosts of the great kings and warriors themselves. Among them was the ghost of Agamemnon, High King of the Greek forces during the Trojan war.

"My lord, king of us all!" Odysseus cried. "You are here!"

As soon as he had tasted the sheep's blood, Agamemnon recognized Odysseus. He tried to lift his arms to embrace him, but there was little strength or power left in his ghostly being.

Odysseus wept tears of pity. Until now he had not known that Agamemnon had died. Now they sat and talked with one another—the living man on one side of the trench, and the ghost of the mighty king on the other.

"What fate brought you here?" asked Odysseus. "Did you drown in a terrible storm at sea? Did an enemy strike you down in some great fight?"

Agamemnon told Odysseus that he had been slain by his own queen.

"But you will not meet the same end, Odysseus," the ghost of Agamemnon assured him. "Your wife, Penelope, is loyal to you. She is a most admirable woman. When you left her, she was little more than a girl. When you return, she and your son will be waiting to embrace you and work with you on your farm."

As Odysseus and the spirit of Agamemnon sat weeping and talking, the ghosts of warriors came and sat with them, warriors who had fought valiantly in the Trojan war. Among them was great Achilles, the bravest of all the Greeks.

"Odysseus, what a daring thing you do now," said Achilles. "Why have you traveled here to be with the ghosts of the dead?"

Odysseus told Achilles and the others about his journey and how he had come to meet with the ghost of Tiresias. He praised Achilles, calling him a prince among the dead.

"Ah, perhaps," said Achilles, "but I would rather be a poor man's servant in the world of the living than a king of kings in the Land of the Dead."

The ghosts of other dead warriors each

told Odysseus their sad tales. And to each ghost, Odysseus gave news about the living.

Then Odysseus saw Tantalus, a king whose great pride had angered the gods. Their punishment for him was eternal hunger and thirst. Tantalus was forced to stand in water up to his chin, with fruit trees drooping overhead, their branches laden with pears, apples, and figs.

Whenever Tantalus lowered his head to drink the water, the water dried up. When he reached up to clutch the fruit, the wind blew the branches into the air.

Next Odysseus saw Sisyphus, a cruel king whom the gods had condemned to forever roll a huge rock uphill. Every time Sisyphus reached the top of the hill, the rock rolled back down the slope, and Sisyphus had to start all over again.

Odysseus then saw the mighty Heracles. The great warrior stared into the distance, holding his bow in his hands, his arrow on the string. For all time he would stand poised to take aim.

As Odysseus looked through the mist for the spirits of more heroes, he saw that thousands of ghosts were moving slowly toward him. Their voices were soft at first. Then they grew louder and louder. The spirits were crowding close around Odysseus, crying out for his help.

Odysseus felt a wave of panic. In terror, he turned and fled from the spirits of the dead. His men followed him back through Persephone's grove until they came to their ship.

Odysseus led the way on board and ordered the Greeks to set sail at once.

The men rowed swiftly across the river of Oceanus. They kept rowing until they felt a breeze and opened their sails.

As dawn's rosy light glittered on the wine-dark sea, Odysseus finally caught his breath. His mind roamed over the past year—the nightmare of the cannibal giants, the long stay in Circe's palace, and his visit to the haunted realm of Hades and Persephone.

Odysseus grieved for his dead mother and felt more anxious than ever to see his father before the old man also died. More than anything, he longed to be reunited with his loving wife and son before harm came to them.

Odysseus' heart ached almost more

than he could bear. Still, he rejoiced that he was in the world of the living and not trapped forever in the dark Land of the Dead.

Book Three

SIRENS AND
SEA MONSTERS

THE LAND OF THE LIVING

Thousands of wailing ghosts moved toward Odysseus. Their anguished cries echoed through the fog. Odysseus and his men began to run. They ran for their lives, fleeing from the dead. . . .

"Land ahead!" one of Odysseus' men called.

Odysseus woke from his nightmare. He had fallen asleep on the deck of his ship. He had been dreaming of his visit to the spirit world ruled by Hades and Persephone. Now in the distance he could see the island of Circe, the enchantress.

I will tell Circe all that I saw and heard in the Land of the Dead, he thought. *Then surely she will help us find our way home to Ithaca.*

For twelve long years, Odysseus had yearned to return to the Greek island of Ithaca and be reunited with his beloved wife and son. During that time, he and his men had fought in the Trojan War. They had battled the Cyclops, a one-eyed monster. They had escaped cannibal giants, losing all but one of their ships. Odysseus had charmed the wily enchantress Circe, and he and his men had now survived a journey to the Land of the Dead—a journey from which no mortal had ever before returned alive.

As they sailed now toward Circe's sunlit island, the Greeks cheered. The island was covered with beautiful green forests and ringed by rocky shores.

Birds sang in the trees as the Greeks anchored their ship. But as the sun went down and they dragged themselves ashore, a great weariness overtook them. Each man collapsed to the sand, too exhausted to speak.

Lying on the cool beach, Odysseus stared up at the moon and stars. He pushed away all his memories of the Land of the Dead. He felt the soft breezes and listened to the waves lap the shore. The world of the living seemed an extraordinary place indeed.

❖　❖　❖

As rosy-fingered dawn spread over the island, Odysseus opened his eyes.

He saw Circe emerge from her palace. She was dressed in a beautiful gown of rainbow colors. Her handmaidens trailed behind her in the fresh morning air, carrying trays of meat, bread, and wine.

Odysseus jumped to his feet and awakened his men. Then he hurried to greet the goddess. Though the enchantress had once tried to harm him and his men, she was now their friend and protector.

"Greetings!" Odysseus called.

"Welcome, my brave friends!" said

Circe, smiling. "You have done what no other mortals have ever done. You have traveled to the Land of the Dead and returned. When you die, others will say that you have died twice."

"Yes, we are grateful to the gods for our safe journey back to your island," Odysseus said. "We pray that you will now help us find our way home to Ithaca."

"Indeed I will," said Circe. "But today you must rest, for you have a long, hard voyage ahead of you. Feast and drink and celebrate your return. Then tomorrow, when the dawn breaks, you shall set sail for Ithaca."

The men cheered. They were famished and thirsty and delighted to spend the day in the company of Circe and her lovely handmaidens.

All morning and all afternoon, Odysseus and his men feasted and drank wine. When the sun finally set and darkness covered the island, the men lay down in the hollow of their ship and fell fast sleep.

Odysseus himself did not rest. Circe took him by the hand and led him into the moonlit forest. Together they sat in the shadows beneath a towering oak.

"Tell me of your journey, Odysseus," Circe said. "What did you see in the Land of the Dead? What did you learn there?"

Odysseus told Circe about his journey to the gray kingdom of Hades and Persephone, rulers of the dead. He told her about the spirits who had come forth, begging for blood so they might be restored to life.

"Among them was my mother," he said sorrowfully. "She died of grief waiting for me to come home to Ithaca. She told me that my father and my wife and son still ache for my return.

"I spoke also with my friend Achilles, who was slain in the Trojan War. I spoke with the High King, Agamemnon. I saw Heracles, Sisyphus, and Tantalus. Finally I spoke with the blind prophet, Tiresias."

"And what did the prophet tell you?" asked Circe.

"He gave me wise counsel and warnings," said Odysseus. "This is what he said: 'On your way home, you will pass the island of the sun god. On this island there are many beautiful sheep and cattle.

Do not let your men touch even one of these creatures. They are much adored by the sun. Anyone who tries to slay them will meet his doom. You alone might escape. But if you do, you will be a broken man. You will find great trouble in your house.'"

Circe sighed. "Yes, those are wise words," she said. "But before you reach the island of the sun god, you must brave other dangers. Listen to me carefully, Odysseus, for I am about to speak of terrible things. But do exactly as I say, and you and your men will find your way home."

CIRCE'S WARNINGS

"*O*dysseus, can you bear to hear what I have to say?" Circe asked him. "Are you prepared to know of the horrors that await you on your journey?"

Odysseus nodded. What could be more

horrible than the Cyclops, or the cannibal giants—or even the spell Circe herself had once cast on his men, turning them into swine?

Circe began: "Soon after you leave my island, you will come upon the island of the Sirens. The Sirens are beautiful women. From a field of flowers, they sing to all sailors who pass their shores."

Odysseus almost laughed. "What threat could these women possibly be to me and my men?" he asked.

"Any sailor who hears the song of the Sirens will forget his homeland, his wife, and his children," said Circe. "The Sirens' lovely singing will lure him to a watery death."

Odysseus smiled and shook his head. He could not believe a simple song could have such power.

"Heed my warning, Odysseus!" said Circe. "The Sirens' shores are littered with the bones of sailors driven mad by their song. You must make your crew plug their ears with beeswax, so none will be able to hear. Else you will all perish!"

"I will order them to do so," Odysseus agreed. "But I myself will listen. I do not believe my will to return home can be broken by a song."

"Then you alone may hear the Sirens," said Circe. "But first your men must tie your hands and your feet to the mast of the ship, or you will surely hurl yourself into the sea. Tell your men that even if you plead with them to loosen your bonds, they must not. Will you swear to do that?"

Odysseus nodded.

"Once you have sailed past the Sirens, you will see two sea paths," said Circe. "One path will lead you between the Wandering Rocks. The Wandering

Rocks are gigantic boulders that pound against one another with terrific fury. No living thing—not even a dove on her way to Zeus—can pass between them without being crushed.

"The waves that foam about the Wandering Rocks are filled with the wreckage of ships and the bodies of sailors. Only Jason and his Argonauts have survived them, but that was because the goddess Hera loved Jason and protected him."

"I fear we cannot depend upon protection from the gods," said Odysseus.

"Tell me, Circe, what is the other path?"

"The other path leads between two sea cliffs," said Circe. "One cliff is quite low. There, under a great fig tree, dwells the deadly whirlpool monster, Charybdis. Any ship that sails near Charybdis is sucked to the black bottom of the sea. Even Poseidon himself cannot save mortal sailors from the monster whirlpool."

"And what of the other cliff?" asked Odysseus. "What danger lies on its shore?"

"High on the side of the second cliff is a dark cave," said Circe. "In the cave dwells the monster Scylla. She yelps like a small hound. But in truth she is a terrible beast. Even the gods and goddesses cannot look upon her without being sickened."

"Why is she so terrible?" asked Odysseus.

"Scylla is a monster with six huge, hideous heads," said Circe. "Her six mouths are filled with razor-sharp teeth. In an instant, the monster can devour six men. All day, Scylla sits inside her cave, gazing greedily over the sea with her twelve eyes. Whenever a ship sails by, she strikes with all her heads and snatches six sailors from the deck. In no time, she rips her poor victims to pieces."

Odysseus stared at the enchantress. "Then the choice you give me is impossible," he said. "Either we are drowned by the whirlpool monster or we die in the jaws of the six-headed beast."

"The choice is this," Circe said. "If you sail close to the monster whirlpool, you will all die. But if you sail close to Scylla, only six will be lost."

Odysseus closed his eyes. He had already seen dozens of his men die hideous deaths. Some had been eaten by the monstrous Cyclops. Others had been speared alive by cannibal giants. How could he bear to see more slaughtered?

"I counsel you to take the course that leads past the monster Scylla," said Circe. "Do not try to fight her. You will lose six men. But if you sail swiftly enough past the monster, you will lose *only* six. The rest will have a chance to escape."

Odysseus was silent for a moment. He could hardly bear to follow Circe's counsel. "How can I knowingly sacrifice my men to such a hideous death?" he asked. "How can I choose which six will die?"

"It is not in your power to choose who shall die," said Circe. "The monster will make the choice for you. Perhaps she will even choose *you*."

Odysseus shook his head. "No. I will kill her before she touches *any* of us," he said.

"Do not be so proud, Odysseus!" Circe said. "You are only a mortal. No mortal—not even you—can defeat Scylla. While you waste time attacking her with your sword, she will devour another six men.

"You must row your ship at full speed! And shout a prayer to Scylla's mother, asking for help. Only she can stop her savage daughter from devouring more men."

Before Odysseus could protest further, Circe went on.

"If you escape from the monster, it will be time to heed the warnings of Tiresias," Circe said. "For soon you will come to the island of Helios, the sun god. There you will see seven herds of cattle and seven flocks of sheep.

"There are fifty beasts in each herd. They are tended by two fair nymphs, daughters of Helios. The sheep and cattle never give birth. They never die. But if any of your men so much as touches them, all your crew will perish. You yourself might escape, but you will have a sad and terrible time when you return home to your island. Your wife and son will suffer also."

Odysseus stood up. The thought that his family might be in danger kindled his desire to start for home at once. "Thank you for your help," he said to Circe. "I promise to heed your warnings."

"Good," she said. "I have told you all that you need to know. Your path will be dangerous indeed. But if you do as I say, you will find your way home. Go now, for the dawn is almost upon us."

Odysseus looked around at the forest. A misty golden-pink light filtered through the trees. A breeze made the leaves quiver and dance. Birds began to sing.

When Odysseus turned back to the enchantress, she was gone.

"Circe!" he called.

She did not answer. She had slipped away into the dawn's rosy light.

THREE

SONG OF THE SIRENS

*O*dysseus was eager to set sail. As he hurried back to the shore, Circe's words echoed in his ears: *Your path will be dangerous indeed. But if you do as I say, you will find your way home.*

Odysseus boarded his ship and commanded his men to cast off at once.

The Greeks stumbled from their sleep and took their places at the oars of the black vessel. As Odysseus was about to raise anchor, Circe's handmaidens appeared on the beach. They carried food and wine for the voyage.

The men happily loaded their gifts onto the ship. Then they bade farewell to the fair maidens and pushed off from the shore.

As the ship sailed away from land, Odysseus stared wistfully at the island of the mysterious enchantress. For the past twelve months, Circe had controlled his fate: she had changed his men into swine and back again. She had sent him on an unfathomable journey into the Land of the Dead. She had armed him with prophecies and warnings for his dangerous voyage home.

Even now he could feel her presence as gentle breezes carried his ship across the waves.

❖   ❖   ❖

As his ship sailed onto the open sea, Odysseus thought of Circe's warnings and the dangers he and his men would soon face.

It is not fair, he thought, *that I should know what horrors await us, while my men know nothing.*

Odysseus stood up and called for his crew to listen.

"Friends!" he said. "Circe has told me much about the journey ahead. Now you shall hear her warnings as well. We will soon approach the island of the Sirens. The Sirens are beautiful women who sing from a field of flowers near the sea."

The men laughed, certain they had nothing to fear from lovely singers.

"Take heed," said Odysseus. "Circe has

warned me that any man who hears the song of the Sirens will drown himself trying to get to them. You must plug your ears so that you cannot hear the enchanting song. I alone may listen, but only if you bind my hands and feet so tightly to the mast of the ship that I cannot break loose. If I beg you to set me free, you must bind me tighter still."

As Odysseus spoke, the wind picked up, filling the sail and carrying the black ship faster and faster across the waves. Then, just as suddenly, the wind ceased. The water grew ominously still.

The men looked about with fear.

"Where is the breeze?" one whispered.

"There is not a ripple on the waves," said another. "What has become of the wind?"

"We must be nearing the island of the Sirens," Odysseus said. "Quick! Let down the sail and stow it away! Be silent. Be swift."

The men did as Odysseus commanded. They lowered the sail and stowed it in the hold. Then they picked up their oars and rowed silently through the eerie, still waters.

While the men rowed, Odysseus grabbed a wheel of beeswax. He held the wax in the sun until it was soft, then cut it into many small pieces. He molded the pieces with his fingers, then handed two to each man.

"Use these to keep the song of the Sirens from reaching your ears," he said. "And then you must bind me to the mast."

The men sealed their ears with the wax. Then they took long cords of rope and tied Odysseus to the mast of the ship. They tied the knots so tightly that no man could loosen them.

The Greeks then picked up their oars again and began to row.

As the black ship moved closer to the island, Odysseus began to hear singing waft through the mist. The sound was more beautiful than he had even imag-ined—high, sweet, and lilting. The words of the Sirens floated on the soft wind:

> *Harken, brave Odysseus,*
> *Listen to us now!*
> *No one can pass our island without staying*
> *To hear our song.*
> *He who listens will be all the wiser,*
> *He who listens*
> *Will discover the secrets of the gods.*

The ship sailed closer and closer to the

shore. Through the mist beyond the still waters, Odysseus saw two lovely women in a flowery meadow.

To his amazement, he saw that the women had wings like birds. Their feathers were translucent in the early morning light.

Odysseus felt an unbearable longing to be with the beautiful creatures. He yearned to spend the rest of his life with them.

As his ship drew closer, Odysseus saw heaps of bleached bones around the bird women. He saw the rotten skin of decaying bodies. He knew he was looking at the remains of sailors who had been enchanted by the Sirens.

But even such a ghastly sight did not keep Odysseus from yearning to throw himself into the sea and swim to the island.

As the Sirens sang their sweet song over and over, Odysseus nearly went mad. He twisted and turned, trying to break free from his bonds.

His men quickened their rowing. Two of them bound Odysseus with more ropes. They rowed faster and faster over the still waters. As they rowed, the song of the Sirens grew fainter.

Odysseus strained to hear the lovely singing as it faded away in the distance. His heart was filled with grief as it grew softer and softer . . . until finally it was gone and all was silent again.

Suddenly the wind picked up. Waves rippled and rolled. Seagulls swooped and cawed.

Odysseus' grief turned to joy. He began to laugh. He was safe! His men were safe! The song of the Sirens was behind them, and they were all safe and well.

THE WHIRLPOOL MONSTER

*W*hen Odysseus' men saw him laughing, they pulled the wax from their ears.

"Untie the ropes!" Odysseus ordered them. "Set me free!"

As his men untied Odysseus, he thanked them.

"I am grateful to you all," he said. "I have heard the song of the Sirens, and I have survived."

The men asked him to describe the beautiful singing. But before Odysseus could speak, he heard a deep rumbling in the distance.

Everyone looked toward the sound. The sea had grown eerily dark. Huge ripples began to rock the ship from side to side.

The rumbling grew louder and louder

until it was a deafening roar. Waves billowed and broke with great force against the ship's hull.

Only Odysseus understood what was happening. His ship and all aboard it were being pulled into the whirlpool of Charybdis.

"Row! Row for your lives!" Odysseus said.

But Odysseus' men shouted in fear and threw down their oars. The ship began to spin in the sea.

Odysseus knew that to escape the whirlpool, he must steer the ship swiftly and steadily toward the cave of the monstrous Scylla. But he could not bear to tell his men the horror that awaited them there.

Instead, Odysseus went around the deck, urging each man not to surrender to fear.

"We have had great trials," he told them, "but we escaped the monstrous Cyclops. We survived the enchantment of Circe. We journeyed to the Land of the Dead and returned unharmed. Pick up your oars now! Row swiftly! Whatever is to come, we must face it with courage!"

Odysseus' heart was heavy as he spoke to his men. He alone knew that at least six of them would soon die hideously in the jaws of the monster Scylla.

Ignorant of their fate and heartened by their leader's words, the Greeks picked up their oars again and began rowing through the wildly rushing waters.

As the helmsman struggled to hold the ship steady, the whirlpool's roar grew unbearably loud. Ferocious waves crashed over the ship.

Soon Odysseus saw a towering cliff looming ahead. The cliff seemed to reach to heaven itself—its peak lost in a cloud. No man could climb to its top, for the cliff's steep sides were as smooth as marble.

Near the cliff's summit was a dark cave. *The home of Scylla, the six-headed monster,* Odysseus thought with dread.

Again Odysseus chose not to tell his men about the monster waiting in her lair. If they knew, their courage would leave them and they would cease to row—and all would be lost in the whirlpool of Charybdis.

Better six shall die than all, Odysseus thought bitterly.

So again, he urged his men to summon their courage:

"Do as I say—trust in Zeus—row with all your might! Steer close to the tall cliff that disappears into the clouds."

Odysseus tried to speak calmly. But he was enraged that six of his comrades were about to die. His fury grew until it led him to make a rash decision: he would defy the counsel of Circe. He would slay the monster before she devoured even one of his men.

Odysseus strapped on his armor. He seized two long spears. Gripping a spear in each hand, he stared up at the looming gray cliff.

Mist partially covered the mouth of Scylla's cave. The cave was so high that even the best warrior could not send an arrow or spear inside it. Odysseus would have to wait for the monster to emerge.

As his men rowed furiously through the dark sea, Odysseus listened for the puppylike yelps of the monster. He waited to see her six long necks and her hideous heads with their rows of gleaming teeth.

He stood on the foredeck of the black ship, ready to slay her.

SCYLLA

As the Greeks drew closer and closer to Scylla's lair, Odysseus glared fiercely at her mist-shrouded cave.

But suddenly Odysseus forgot all about Scylla, for his attention was seized by the roaring sea. Just off the bow of the ship, the whirlpool monster, Charybdis, was sucking up tons of black water and vomiting it out.

Spray from the monster's mouth rained down on the deck. The sea around the ship bubbled and churned like water roiling in a giant cauldron.

Odysseus could see into the center of the whirlpool—a deep cavity filled with black ooze and mud. If his ship veered even slightly toward the swirling water, it would surely be sucked down into the darkness.

Odysseus dropped his spears. "Hold our course!" he shouted to his men. "Row with all your might toward the towering cliff!"

Odysseus' men cried out in fear. At that moment, Scylla stuck her hideous heads out of her cave.

In an instant, the monster's six long necks swooped down toward the sea. She grabbed Odysseus' best warriors in her six mouths. As she lifted the helpless Greeks high into the air, the men writhed like fish caught by a giant fisherman.

Odysseus saw bloody hands and feet

dangling from Scylla's mouths. He heard the men scream his name, begging for help.

The hideous monster devoured her victims before Odysseus' eyes. It was the most terrible sight of his life.

Odysseus knew now that Circe had been right. He had been foolish to think he could slay the monster. The only way to save the rest of his men was to speed away from her as swiftly as possible.

"Row! Row!" he shouted. "If you value your lives, row with all your strength!"

The men rowed frantically past the tall cliff. With Odysseus urging them on, they sped through the channel, until they were finally safe from both sea monsters, Scylla and Charybdis.

ISLAND OF THE SUN GOD

Odysseus stood at the helm of his ship. He stared into the churning sea behind him, horrified by the cruel slaughter of his men. Their screams still rang in his ears. The sight of their bloody, struggling limbs was imprinted on his memory forever.

But Odysseus knew that the rest of his men needed him now—their fear and trembling forced him to rally himself and take command.

"Row on!" he said, lifting his head in the wind. "Do not look back! Do not think about what you have seen, or we will never find our way home!"

Too stunned even to speak, the Greeks picked up their oars. Like obedient children, they rowed on.

The black ship sped across the wine-dark

sea. Soon the Greeks saw a sun-drenched island in the distance. They heard the lowing of cattle and bleating of sheep.

Odysseus' men rejoiced at the sounds. After their terrible ordeal, they yearned for rest and shelter and food.

"Soon we will feast on beef and mutton!" they exclaimed.

Odysseus did not rejoice. He knew that he and his men were approaching the island of the sun god. He remembered the stern warnings of the prophet Tiresias and the counsel of Circe.

"Heed what I tell you," he said to his

crew. "I know you crave food and rest. But the island ahead belongs to Helios, the sun god. We cannot seek provisions there. I have been warned by the prophet Tiresias and by Circe. They told me that the sun god adores his cattle and sheep, and that if one of you even dares touch them, you all will die."

Upon hearing these words, the men nearly collapsed with weariness and anguish.

"Then let us die there," said one, "for we will surely die at sea if we do not eat and rest soon."

"Listen to me," Odysseus said. "If we stop now, all our trials—all our triumphs and all our losses—will have been for naught. We must move past this island. We must keep rowing."

The men protested again. When Odysseus would not hear their pleas, Eurylochus, the second in command on the ship, shouted at him in anger.

"Odysseus, you are too strong!" he said. "You are made of iron; the rest of us are not! We are only human. These men need rest from their labor and time to mourn their losses. They cannot row through the night. Let us heed the darkness. Let us stop on the island to rest. We will cook our own food and sleep on the sand. We will set sail again at dawn without even laying eyes upon the precious cattle and sheep of the sun god."

The men cheered the plan put forth by Eurylochus, but Odysseus' heart was filled with dread. Even though the plan seemed sound, Odysseus felt as if some angry god were plotting against him. Still, he knew there was no way now he could convince his men to row on.

"You force me to surrender to your

will," he said. "I cannot fight you all. But if we do as Eurylochus asks, you must swear an oath—you must promise not to touch a single head of the sun god's cattle or sheep. You must be satisfied only with the food that Circe has given us."

The men swore to do as Odysseus commanded. Soon they dropped anchor in a sheltered bay of Helios' island.

Near the shore, the Greeks found a spring of fresh water. They set up camp and made a meal from Circe's gifts of meat and bread and wine.

Once the men had satisfied their hunger and thirst, painful memories swept over them. They wept for their six comrades eaten alive by the monster Scylla. Her victims had been the strongest and best of Odysseus' warriors.

The Greeks wept also for the others on their voyage who had been slain by monsters and giants. They mourned their losses deep into the night, until sleep mercifully overcame them.

SEVEN

THE TEMPEST

 $\mathcal{I}$ n the darkest period of the night, just before the dawn, Zeus sent a terrible storm to the island of the sun god. Fierce winds shook the trees. Cold rain poured down from the heavens.

The Greeks scrambled into a huge cave near the shore. They huddled together, listening to the roar of the storm. At the first light of dawn, as the wind and rain raged on, Odysseus ordered his men to drag their ship ashore and pull it into the cave with them.

Once the ship was safely in the cave, Odysseus gathered his crew around him.

"Friends, we cannot leave the island this morning," he told them. "So I command you again: do not touch the sheep or cows that belong to Helios, the sun god. He sees all and he hears all. He will know at once if you try to feast upon his treasures. We have all the food we need now in our ship. As soon as this tempest ends, we will sail on."

The Greek warriors promised to do as Odysseus commanded. But day after day, fierce storm winds from the south and east pummeled the sun god's island. The days grew into weeks, and still the tempest did not end. Never did the storm cease long enough for the Greeks to set sail.

For over a month, Odysseus and his men remained stranded on the island. At first, they ate only the food given them by

Circe. But when those provisions were gone, the men were forced to roam the stormy coast, spearing fish and birds and anything else they might eat.

As the tempest raged on and on, Odysseus and his men could not find enough food. Each day, they ate less. Each day, they grew weaker. Hunger gnawed at their bellies and despair seized their souls.

Odysseus grew more and more frightened that the men would lose control of themselves. He feared their hunger would eventually drive them to slay the cattle and sheep of the sun god. And he knew that the sun god's anger would bring death upon them all.

Early one morning while the others were still sleeping, Odysseus slipped from the cave. He ran through the storm and took shelter in a solitary outcropping of rock near the shore.

Odysseus knelt on the ground. He raised his arms and called out to the gods and goddesses of Mount Olympus. He begged them to show pity: "Give us courage to withstand our hunger and despair," he prayed. "Send us fair weather so we might sail away soon. Help us follow the counsel of Tiresias and over-come temptation. . . ."

As Odysseus prayed, a great drowsi-ness overtook him. He closed his eyes. His head fell forward and he sank into a deep, dreamless sleep.

PUNISHMENT OF THE GODS

Odysseus woke with a start. He could tell from the morning light that several hours had passed since he had fallen asleep. With a feeling of dread, he leapt from the ground and started running back to his men.

As Odysseus neared the cave, his heart sank. The smell of burning meat filled the air.

Odysseus was seized with rage and horror. Rushing into the cave, he grabbed the first man he came upon. "What have you done?" he demanded. "Have you disobeyed my orders and defied the gods?"

"We were following Eurylochus!" the man said. "He told us that starvation was the most terrible of all deaths! He urged us to slay the cattle of the sun god! He said we could appease Helios by building a great temple in his honor when we return to Ithaca."

Odysseus nearly wept with despair.

"We were so hungry, we could not stop ourselves," the man said. "We killed the best of the cattle and roasted them over the fire."

Odysseus cried out in agony. He fell to his knees and called to the gods: "Zeus and all immortal gods, why did you allow me to fall asleep? I begged you to give my men strength and courage! Now they have defied my command and slain the cattle of Helios! Have mercy on us! Have mercy on us all!"

But Odysseus knew his prayers were in vain. The rage of Helios was surely more powerful than the anguished pleas of a mere mortal. Odysseus imagined that the sun god might threaten never to shine upon the earth again unless the gods helped him take his revenge.

Odysseus rose to his feet and looked about the cave. The scene was horrible and unnatural. The hides of the slain cattle crawled across the ground. On the spits, the roasting meat bellowed like living beasts.

Odysseus' men cowered before him. As he glared at their terrified faces, the rage drained from his heart. It was too late for rage now. The cattle of Helios were dead, and the men who had slain them would soon die also. Nothing less, Odysseus knew, would appease the sun god's anger.

❖   ❖   ❖

For the next six days, as the winds blew harshly outside the cave, Odysseus' men feasted on the sun god's cattle.

Finally, on the seventh day, the storm abruptly ceased.

At Odysseus' command, the Greeks pulled their ship from its shelter and pushed off into the water. A gentle west wind caught their sail, and they headed once again for the distant shores of Ithaca.

For a time, it seemed possible that the sun god's rage had been forgotten. But once the black ship had sailed onto the open sea, Odysseus' worst fears were realized. Helios had indeed turned all the other gods against the Greeks. And together, the gods took their revenge.

First, mighty Zeus sent a black storm cloud across the sky, darkening the waters and turning the day into night.

Then Poseidon, god of the seas, sent tumultuous waves crashing over the sides of the ship.

Then Aeolus, the wind god, sent a howling wind that blew with such fury that it cracked the ship's mast. The mast and rigging fell on top of the helmsman, crushing his skull.

Zeus shook the sky with thunder and hurled down a blazing bolt of lightning. The lightning struck the ship's hull, spinning it around and around on the water. All of Odysseus' men were thrown from the deck into the dark, angry sea.

Watching helplessly from the ship, Odysseus saw his men tossed on the waves like sea birds. He watched as, one by one, they sank beneath the water and drowned.

Finally all of Odysseus' men had disappeared under the waves. And Odysseus was completely and terribly alone.

ONLY ODYSSEUS

Odysseus clung to the lurching ship until the storm began to rip it apart. Then, as the rest of the ship was torn to splinters, he lashed the mast and keel together, making a raft.

For hours, Odysseus clung to the raft for dear life as wild winds tossed him over the waves.

Darkness soon covered the ocean. As the sea grew calmer, Odysseus feared his raft might be drifting back toward the cave of Scylla and the whirlpool of Charybdis. All through the night he prayed to the gods to spare him from the monsters.

But as dawn broke, Odysseus saw Scylla's cliff rising from the sea—and he heard the awful roar of Charybdis. He could feel the black waters of Charybdis' whirlpool begin to pull at his raft.

Odysseus' prayers had been in vain. His raft was being sucked into the black, swirling mouth of Charybdis. His body would soon join those of all the other sailors who had drowned in the terrible whirlpool.

But just as he was about to be sucked into the monster's mouth, a mighty wave swept Odysseus from his raft. The wave carried him away from the whirlpool— over the sea—onto the shores of Scylla's cliff.

Odysseus flung himself from the water and grabbed the trunk of a huge fig tree. He clung to the tree like a bat. Holding on with all his strength, he waited for the whirlpool monster to vomit up his raft.

Finally the raft was hurled from the black abyss and sent swirling over the waves. When it was within reach, Odysseus let go of the tree and plunged into the sea.

He grabbed the edge of the raft and heaved himself aboard. Then he began rowing madly with his hands. He rowed and rowed. He rowed away from Charybdis. He rowed past the cliff of

Scylla. He rowed until he was safe from both dreaded sea monsters.

※　　※　　※

For nine days and nine nights, Odysseus drifted on his raft. He had no food and no water. He had no idea where he was going—or how he would ever get home.

As he drifted over the open sea, he mourned the loss of all his comrades. He grieved for the family he feared he would never see again.

Finally, on the tenth day, the waves tossed Odysseus and his raft onto the shore of a mysterious island.

T E N

CALYPSO

Odysseus lay on the sandy beach, tired to the bone and filled with despair. He had not slept in ten days. Now that he was safe on shore, he was tortured by visions of his men dangling from the mouths of the monstrous Scylla. Over and over he saw his comrades devoured by monsters or drowned in the waves, bobbing like sea birds, then vanishing, one by one. Friends and warriors, men he had journeyed with for twelve long years—they were now gone. He had lost them all.

Only the last words of Tiresias, the blind prophet, were yet to come to pass: *"You alone might escape. But if you do, you will be a broken man. You will find great trouble in your house."*

Odysseus could not bear the thought that Penelope, his wife, and Telemachus, his son, might be suffering in Ithaca. He desperately wanted to protect them. In spite of his despair, he still felt a fierce determination to return home.

Nearly blind with exhaustion and grief, Odysseus pulled himself up from the sand and began walking in search of help.

He had not gone far before he came upon four streams. The bubbling waters wound through lush green meadows filled with violets, parsley, and wild celery.

Just beyond the streams was a rocky hillside. Set deep in the rocks was a huge cave. Long vines trailed around the mouth of the cave. Clusters of ripe grapes hung from the vines.

Beautiful trees grew along the path that led to the cave—alder, aspen, and sweet-smelling cypress. Owls, falcons, and sea ravens had built their nests in the boughs of the trees.

Odysseus smelled the sweet scent of burning cedar and sandalwood.

Like someone lost in a dream, Odysseus stumbled slowly toward the cave's entrance. When he peered inside, he saw a great fire blazing in the hearth.

Beside the hearth sat a beautiful woman

at a loom. She shone with the light of a goddess. She was weaving and singing in a lovely voice.

As her song ended, the goddess turned and smiled at Odysseus.

"Hello, Odysseus," she said. "I am Calypso, daughter of Atlas. Hermes told me that you might come."

Odysseus was surprised that the goddess knew his name. But he was too weary even to speak.

Calypso looked at Odysseus for a long time. Then she continued in her calm, lovely voice: "I know what has happened to you," she said. "Your men killed the cattle of the sun god. In a rage, Helios threatened to take away his light forever, from men and from the gods. Zeus and the other gods of Mount Olympus were forced to take revenge against you. Zeus smashed your ship with a thunderbolt and hurled your warriors into the sea. They drowned before your eyes."

Odysseus nodded.

"You must be very tired, Odysseus," Calypso said kindly. "Come inside. Rest here in my home."

Without a word, Odysseus stepped

into the cave of the beautiful goddess.

He stumbled to the hearth and lay down close to the fire. After his terrible journey, he was indeed a broken man. His heart and body ached almost more than he could bear.

As Odysseus stared at the fire in the hearth, the goddess began to sing her song again. Odysseus was reminded of the singing of the Sirens. But Calypso's song did not make him go mad or lure him to a watery death.

Instead, as Odysseus listened, all the pain and horror of his journey slowly dissolved around him. He felt peaceful and calm for the first time in many weeks.

Odysseus closed his eyes. And in the peaceful warmth of Calypso's cave, he finally fell asleep.

Don't miss the exciting conclusion to
Odysseus' story in:

TALES FROM THE
ODYSSEY
PART TWO

including:

BOOK FOUR
THE GRAY-EYED GODDESS

BOOK FIVE
RETURN TO ITHACA

BOOK SIX
THE FINAL BATTLE

ABOUT HOMER AND THE ODYSSEY

Long ago, the ancient Greeks believed that the world was ruled by a number of powerful gods and goddesses. Stories about the gods and goddesses are called the Greek myths. The myths were probably first told as a way to explain things in nature—such as weather, volcanoes, and constellations. They were also recited as entertainment.

The first written record of the Greek myths comes from a blind poet named Homer. Homer lived almost three thousand years ago. Many believe that Homer was the author of the world's two most famous epic poems: the *Iliad* and the *Odyssey*. The *Iliad* is the story of the Trojan War. The *Odyssey* tells about the long journey of Odysseus, king of an island called Ithaca. The tale concerns Odysseus' adventures on his way home from the Trojan War.

To tell his tales, Homer seems to have drawn upon a combination of his own imagination and Greek myths that had been passed down by word of mouth. A bit of actual history may have also gone into Homer's stories; there is archaeological evidence to suggest that the story of the Trojan War was based on a war fought about five hundred years before Homer's time.

Over the centuries, Homer's *Odyssey* has greatly influenced the literature of the Western world.

GODS AND GODDESSES OF ANCIENT GREECE

$\mathcal{T}$he most powerful of all the Greek gods and goddesses was Zeus, the thunder god. Zeus ruled the heavens and the mortal world from a misty mountaintop known as Mount Olympus. The main Greek gods and goddesses were all relatives of Zeus. His brother Poseidon was ruler of the seas, and his brother Hades was ruler of the underworld. His wife Hera was queen of the gods and goddesses. Among his many children were the gods Apollo, Mars, and Hermes, and the goddesses Aphrodite, Athena, and Artemis.

The gods and goddesses of Mount Olympus not only inhabited their mountaintop but also visited the earth, involving themselves in the daily activities of mortals such as Odysseus.

THE MAIN GODS
AND GODDESSES
AND PRONUNCIATION
OF THEIR NAMES

Zeus (zyoos), king of the gods, god of thunder

Poseidon (poh-SY-don), brother of Zeus, god of seas and rivers

Hades (HAY-deez), brother of Zeus, king of the Land of the Dead

Hera (HEE-ra), wife of Zeus, queen of the gods and goddesses

Hestia (HES-tee-ah), sister of Zeus, goddess of the hearth

Athena (ah-THEE-nah), daughter of Zeus, goddess of wisdom and war, arts and crafts

Demeter (dee-MEE-tur), goddess of crops and the harvest, mother of Persephone

Aphrodite (ah-froh-DY-tee), daughter of Zeus, goddess of love and beauty

Artemis (AR-tem-is), daughter of Zeus, goddess of the hunt

Ares (AIR-eez), son of Zeus, god of war

Apollo (ah-POL-oh), god of the sun, music, and poetry

Hermes (HUR-meez), son of Zeus, messenger god, a trickster

Hephaestus (heh-FEES-tus), son of Hera, god of the forge

Persephone (pur-SEF-oh-nee), daughter of Zeus, wife of Hades and queen of the Land of the Dead

Dionysus (dy-oh-NY-sus), god of wine and madness

PRONUNCIATION GUIDE TO OTHER PROPER NAMES

Achilles (ah-KIL-eez)

Aeolus (EE-oh-lus)

Agamemnon (ag-ah-MEM-non)

Calypso (Kah-LIP-soh)

Charybdis (Kah-RIB-dis)

Circe (SIR-see)

Cyclops (SY-klops)

Eurylochus (yoo-RIH-loh-kus)

Helios (HE-lee-ohs)

Heracles (HER-ah-kleez)

Ithaca (ITH-ah-kah)

Odysseus (oh-DIS-yoos)

Penelope (pen-EL-oh-pee)

Polyphemus (pah-lih-FEE-mus)

Scylla (SIL-ah)

Sisyphus (SIS-ih-fus)

Tantalus (TAN-tah-lus)

Telemachus (tel-EM-ah-kus)

Tiresias (ty-REE-sih-us)

Trojans (TROH-junz)

A NOTE ON THE SOURCES

$\mathcal{T}$he story of the Odyssey was originally written down in the ancient Greek language. Since that time there have been countless translations of Homer's story into other languages. I consulted a number of English translations, including those written by Alexander Pope, Samuel Butler, Andrew Lang, W.H.D. Rouse, Edith Hamilton, Robert Fitzgerald, Allen Mandelbaum, and Robert Fagles.

Homer's *Odyssey* is divided into twenty-four books. Book One, *The One-Eyed Giant*, was derived from books nine and ten of Homer's *Odyssey*.

The story concerning Odysseus' recruitment for the Trojan War originated with the second-century A.D. writer Hyginus. The account of the Trojan horse was derived from Virgil's *Aeneid*. Apollodorus' account of the fall of Troy mentions that the name of Athena was inscribed on the wooden horse. Book Two, *The Land of the Dead*, is derived from books ten and eleven of Homer's *Odyssey*. The third volume, *Sirens and Sea Monsters*, was derived from book twelve of Homer's *Odyssey*, with details concerning Odysseus' arrival on Calypso's island coming from book five.

ABOUT THE AUTHOR

MARY POPE OSBORNE is the author of the best-selling Magic Tree House series. She has also written many acclaimed historical novels and retellings of myths and folktales, including *Tales from the Odyssey, Part 2*, *Kate and the Beanstalk*, and *New York's Bravest*. She lives with her husband in New York City and Connecticut.

Zeus

Hera

Artemis

Hephaestus

Ares

Apollo

Athena

GODS *and* GODDESSES
of ANCIENT GREECE

Hermes

Dionysus

Aphrodite

Hestia

Demeter

Persephone

Poseidon

Hades